D0970341

This book belongs to:

_____

Copyright © 2006 by Callaway & Kirk Company LLC. All rights reserved.
Published by Callaway & Kirk Company LLC, a division of Callaway Arts & Entertainment.
Miss Spider, Sunny Patch Friends, and all related characters are trademarks and/or
registered trademarks of Callaway & Kirk Company LLC. All rights reserved.

Digital art by Callaway Animation Studios under the direction of David Kirk in collaboration with Nelvana Limited.

This book is based on the TV episode "Cry Buggie," written by Michael Stokes, from the animated TV series
Miss Spider's Sunny Patch Friends on Nick Jr., a Nelvana Limited/Absolute Pictures Limited co-production
in association with Callaway Arts & Entertainment, based on the Miss Spider books by David Kirk.

Nicholas Callaway, President and Publisher
Cathy Ferrara, Managing Editor and Production Director
Toshiya Masuda, Art Director • Nelson Gomez, Director of Digital Services
Joya Rajadhyaksha, Associate Editor • Amy Cloud, Associate Editor
Raphael Shea, Senior Designer • Krupa Jhaveri, Designer
Bill Burg, Digital Artist • Christina Pagano, Digital Artist
Mary Boyer, Digital Artist • Dominique Genereux, Digital Artist

Special thanks to the Nelvana staff, including Doug Murphy, Scott Dyer, Tracy Ewing, Pam Lehn,
Tonya Lindo, Mark Picard, Jane Sobol, Luis Lopez, Eric Pentz, and Georgina Robinson.

Library of Congress Cataloging-in-Publication Data available upon request.

Distributed in the United States by Viking Children's Books.

Callaway Arts & Entertainment, its Callaway logotype,
and Callaway & Kirk Company LLC are trademarks.

ISBN 0-448-44427-5

Visit Callaway Arts & Entertainment at www.callaway.com

10 9 8 7 6 5 4 3 2 1   06 07 08 09 10

Printed in China

Miss
Spider's
SUNNY PATCH FRIENDS

Cry Buggie

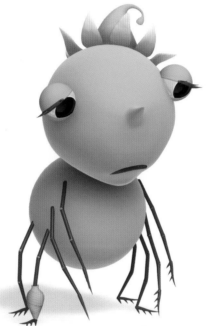

David Kirk

CALLAWAY

NEW YORK

2006

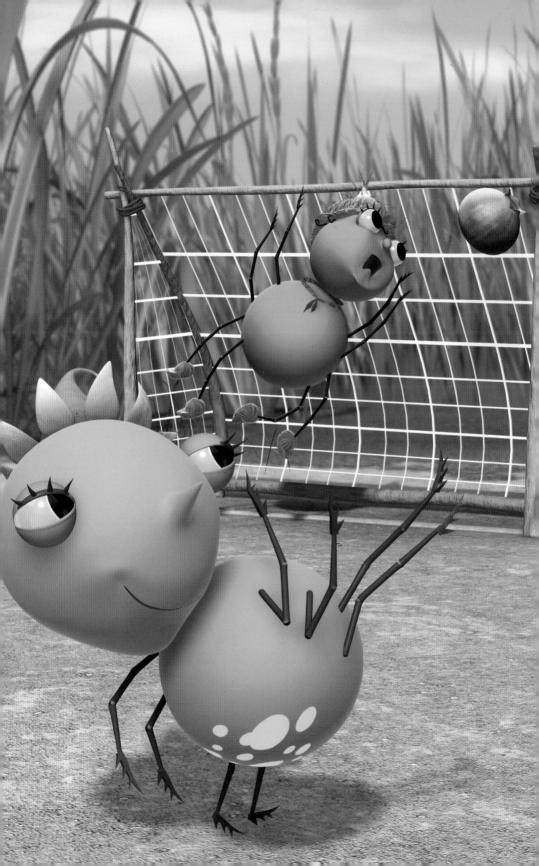

On a sunny summer day in Sunny Patch, Miss Spider's children were playing soccerberry.

"Nothing gets past the Wiggle Wall," said Wiggle. But before he knew it, Squirt kicked the ball into the net.

"GOAL!" everyone yelled.

"Wow, Squirt," Pansy said. "You must be the best soccerberry player in Sunny Patch."

"Try the whole buggy world!" said Dragon proudly.

"You'll be great at the tournament tomorrow," Shimmer said.

They suddenly noticed that Wiggle was still sitting in the net, sniffling.

"It's no buggie-biggie, Wiggle," Shimmer said. "You can't win 'em all."

"Squirt and I can," said Dragon.

"Wiggle is just a cry buggie," said Dragon as they headed home. "Big bugs like me don't cry."

"Never?" Squirt asked.

"Nope, never," Dragon replied.

"Then I don't cry either," Squirt decided.

Later, while everybuggy practiced for the tournament, Squirt tripped as he was rushing to make a goal.

"Whoooaaaa!" he cried.

"I think you sprained your goal-kicking leg, son," Holley said, examining Squirt's ankle.

Squirt's eyes welled up with pain, but then he saw Dragon and forced his tears back.

By nightfall, Squirt's injured ankle had swelled up like a grape.

"Sorry, Sport," said Holley. "There's no way you can play in tomorrow's tournament."

"But I can't let Dragon down!" Squirt wailed. "He said I'm the best player in the whole world."

"You'll still be the best player when your leg heals," Holley comforted.

Squirt fought hard to suppress his sniffles.

"Honey, it's fine to let out your feelings and cry," Miss Spider said.

After his parents left the room, Squirt told himself, "Big bugs don't cry."

The next morning Squirt looked sad as everyone prepared to leave for the tournament.

"Have a good time, everybuggy," he sighed.

"We'll win this one for you," Dragon called as he zoomed off.

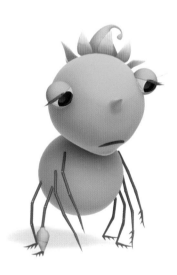

"Ready to go to the tournament?" Miss Spider asked.

"Why should I go?" Squirt asked. "I can't play."

"But you can cheer your brothers and sisters on," Holley reminded him.

"No thanks, Dad," Squirt said, and hobbled up to the bedroom.

quirt finally decided to go outside and watch the game from a branch.

On the field, Pansy kicked the ball hard. It flew into the net.

"GOOAAAL!" Mr. Mantis yelled.

High above, Squirt sighed. He turned around and saw his parents on the branch, too.

"I just came out here to watch the clouds," Squirt said, his lips quivering.

"When a cloud travels it picks up all kinds of things," Miss Spider said, "like water and dust and maybe a bad feeling or two."

"Eventually," Holley continued, "the cloud gets so full that it has to let everything out as . . ."

"Rain," Squirt said, as a few drops began to fall.

"Yes, rain," Holley said. "And just like clouds, bugs need to cry. Big bugs, little bugs—even mom and dad bugs."

At long last Squirt let out his feelings and started to cry.

Gradually, the rain stopped and so did Squirt's tears.

"I feel better now, Mom," he said.

"So does the cloud," said Miss Spider. "Look, it feels so good it's built a . . ."

"Rainbow!" exclaimed Squirt, staring at the bridge of colors over Sunny Patch.

When the three bugs went inside, they were surprised to see that the rest of the family was already home.

"They cancelled the tournament," Pansy explained.

Dragon was sobbing. "I really, really wanted to play! It's not fair!"

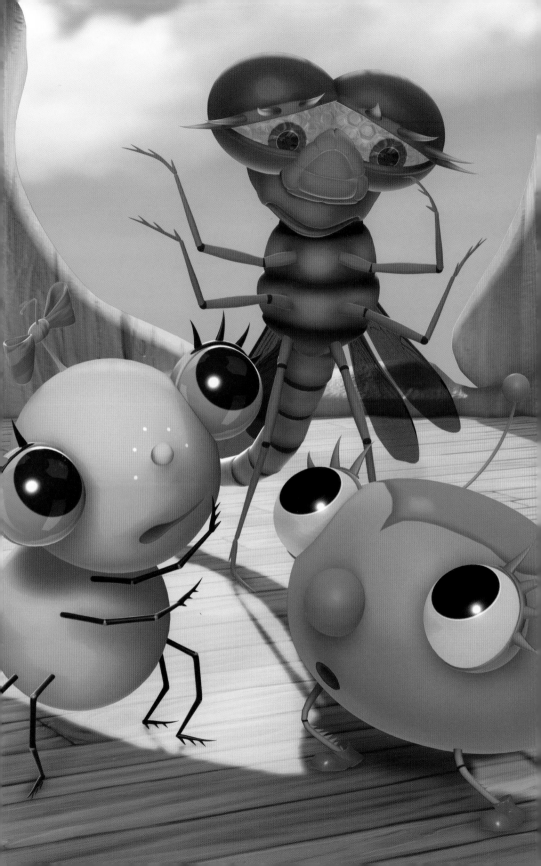

Squirt hobbled over to his older brother. "I know how you feel."

"I'm not really crying," Dragon said, trying to cover up his tears.

"Don't be embarrassed," Squirt smiled. "Big bugs do cry . . . when they need to."